DISNEY
CLASSICS
STORYBOOK TREASURY

DISNEP PRESS

LOS ANGELES · NEW YORK

This book is a gift for:

_____

TABLE OF CONTENTS

"Always let your conscience be your guide."

—The Blue Fairy

PINOCCHIO

ONCE UPON A TIME, there was a friendly cricket named Jiminy. One night, Jiminy Cricket's travels took him to the workshop of an old wood-carver named Geppetto. Ticking clocks, music boxes, and wonderful wooden toys filled the room.

Geppetto was putting the finishing touches on a new puppet.

"I have just the name for you," Geppetto said. "Pinocchio!"

Then he added softly to himself, "He almost looks alive."

That evening at bedtime, Geppetto looked out the window. Twinkling up in the sky was the Wishing Star.

"I wish Pinocchio were a *real* boy," he said.

Soon Geppetto and his cat, Figaro, were fast asleep. Only Jiminy Cricket was still awake.

Suddenly, a bright blue light filled the workshop. The beautiful Blue Fairy appeared. "Good Geppetto," she said gently. "You have given so much happiness to others. You deserve to have your wish come true."

Waving her wand over Pinocchio, she said:

"Little puppet made of pine, wake! The gift of life is thine."

Magically, Pinocchio began to stir. The Blue Fairy asked Jiminy Cricket to be Pinocchio's conscience, to teach him right from wrong.

"Prove yourself brave, truthful, and unselfish, and someday you will be a real boy,"

the Blue Fairy told Pinocchio.

"And remember, Pinocchio, be a good boy and always let your conscience be your guide."

And with that, she disappeared.

When Geppetto woke up, he saw Pinocchio walking and talking! At first he thought he must be dreaming, but then he realized his wish had come true!

Geppetto was so happy, he began to play a merry tune for everyone to dance to.

The next morning, Geppetto sent Pinocchio off to school. But on his way there, a fox called Honest John and a cat named Gideon spotted him skipping along.

"A live puppet without strings!"

Honest John cried.

"I could sell him to Stromboli's show and make lots of money!"

They convinced Pinocchio that becoming an actor would be more fun than going to school. Jiminy tried to stop Pinocchio from going with them, but the little puppet was too excited to listen.

"Jiminy tried to stop Pinocchio . . ."

That night, Pinocchio sang and danced in the puppet show. The audience clapped and cheered with delight. Pinocchio was a star!

After the performance, the little puppet asked to go home.

Stromboli, the owner of the show, roared with anger. He locked Pinocchio in a cage.

"This will be your home now!"

he bellowed.

Suddenly, Jiminy Cricket and the Blue Fairy appeared. "Pinocchio, why didn't you go to school?" the Blue Fairy asked.

The little puppet was afraid to tell the truth, so he lied.

But as soon as he did, his nose began to grow!

"Perhaps you haven't been telling the truth, Pinocchio," the Blue Fairy said. "A lie keeps growing and growing until it's as plain as the nose on your face."

"I'll never lie again,"
the little puppet promised.

The Blue Fairy gently touched Pinocchio's nose with her wand and it turned back to normal. She unlocked the cage, and Pinocchio and Jiminy Cricket ran back to Geppetto's workshop.

"A lie keeps growing and growing . . ."

As he headed home, Pinocchio ran into Honest John and Gideon again. This time, they persuaded Pinocchio that he needed a holiday at a wonderful place called Pleasure Island. They whisked Pinocchio away before Jiminy could catch up to them.

The two villains sold Pinocchio to a wicked coachman, who put him on a coach full of very noisy, naughty boys. Luckily, Jiminy was able to climb onto the coach just as it drove off.

Pleasure Island was like a giant amusement park. The boys could have anything they wanted and be as naughty as they liked. While Pinocchio enjoyed all the ice cream and sweet treats he could eat, Jiminy searched for the little puppet. He was sure something was wrong and wanted to get Pinocchio out of there as soon as possible!

Finally, Jiminy found Pinocchio. He begged the little puppet to leave, but Pinocchio refused to listen.

Jiminy knew he would not be able to change Pinocchio's mind, so he decided to go home on his own. But as he was leaving, he saw the wicked coachman loading crates of donkeys onto a boat.

One of the donkeys was crying and begging to go home to its mother. Jiminy was shocked!

Somehow, all the boys on Pleasure Island were being turned into donkeys!

Jiminy raced off to save Pinocchio. But by the time Jiminy found him, the little puppet had already grown long hairy ears and a tail!

"Come on! Quick!" Jiminy cried. "This way, Pinoke!"

Pinocchio followed Jiminy up a steep cliff. When they reached the top, they jumped into the sea and swam home.

Cold and tired, they finally reached Geppetto's house. But all they found was a note.

Geppetto had gone looking for Pinocchio across the sea and had been swallowed by a big whale named Monstro!

Pinocchio was determined to find his father, no matter how dangerous it would be. So he and Jiminy headed into the sea.

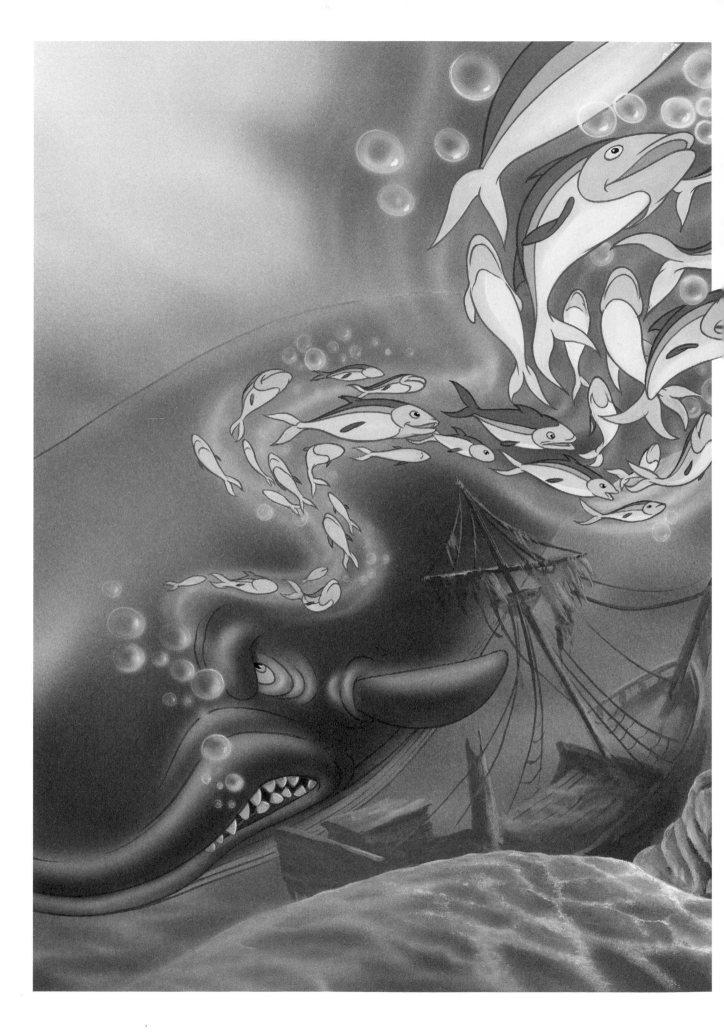

Pinocchio and Jiminy asked the fish and sea horses for help. But as soon as the sea creatures heard Monstro's name, they sped off in terror.

Meanwhile, not too far away, Monstro was waking up from a long sleep.

The whale was so hungry that he gulped down a large school of fish. Without realizing what he'd done, he swallowed Pinocchio, too!

Deep inside the whale's stomach, Geppetto thought sadly of Pinocchio. How he wished he could see his son just one more time.

Just then, Geppetto felt a tug on his fishing line.

It was Pinocchio!

Pinocchio and his father were overjoyed to see each other again. But they still needed to escape the whale's stomach!

Suddenly, Pinocchio had an idea.

"We'll make him sneeze!"

he said excitedly.

Pinocchio and Geppetto built a fire to fill Monstro's stomach with smoke.

"They still needed to escape the whale's stomach!"

Pinocchio's plan worked!

As the air around them filled with clouds of black smoke, Monstro gave an enormous sneeze—and out they all went on a little raft!

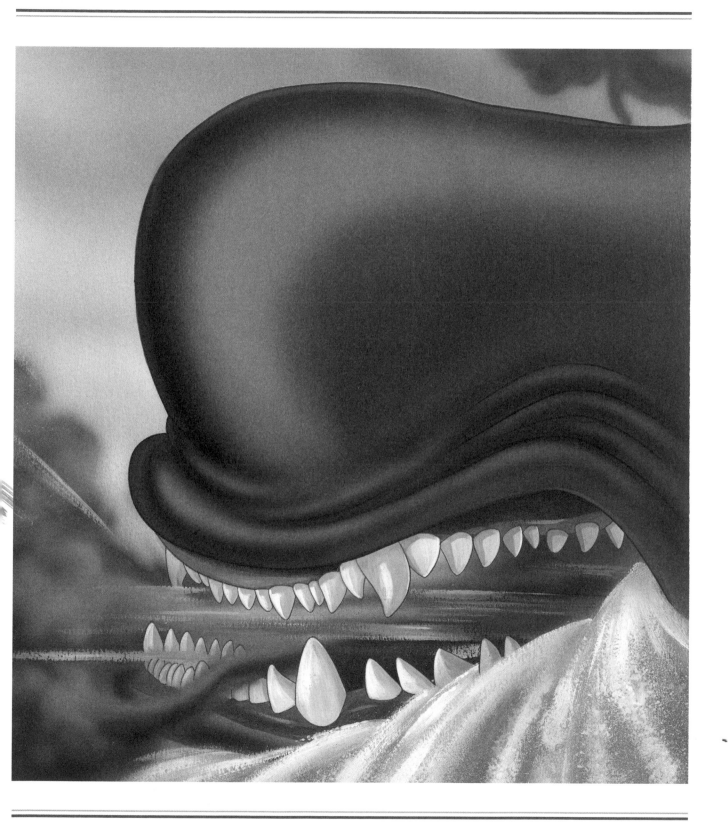

The whale slapped his large tail, creating a big wave. The little raft was smashed to pieces.

Everyone was thrown into the sea. But Geppetto couldn't swim! Pinocchio kept his father afloat and dragged him to shore.

Moments later, Jiminy found Geppetto, Figaro, and Cleo the goldfish safe on the beach.

But the little puppet was lying facedown in the water. He wasn't moving.

Heartbroken, Geppetto took his son home.

Geppetto knelt over Pinocchio and wept. Just then, the Blue Fairy's dazzling light filled the room.

"Prove yourself brave, truthful, and unselfish, and someday you will be a real boy," the Blue Fairy said gently. "Awake, Pinocchio, awake."

Pinocchio blinked his eyes and sat up. He was no longer made of wood. He was a real boy at last!

"Father, I'm alive! See?"

Pinocchio cried out in delight.

Jiminy proudly watched as Pinocchio and his father happily danced together. Now he knew: if you wished upon a star, your dreams really could come true!

"Tonight's my last night in the nursery. I have to grow up tomorrow."

—Wendy

PETER PAN

L ONG AGO IN LONDON, there lived three children: Wendy, John, and Michael Darling.

Each night, Wendy told her brothers stories before bed. John and Michael loved all of Wendy's stories of adventure. But their favorites were about Peter Pan, a boy who lived in a faraway place called Never Land and refused to grow up.

One night, the children's father, Mr. Darling, was quite angry. His sons were pretending to be pirates, and Michael had drawn a treasure map on his father's last clean shirt. Mr. Darling blamed Wendy for filling the boys' heads with stories of Peter Pan.

"This is the last night in the nursery, young lady," Mr. Darling said.

"It's time for you to grow up."

Mrs. Darling tucked the children into bed, and before long, they were fast asleep.

Suddenly, two figures appeared outside the house.

It was Peter Pan and his fairy friend, Tinker Bell!

The Darlings' nursery was a familiar place to Peter. He liked to sit in the shadows and listen to Wendy's stories about Never Land.

"He liked to sit in the shadows . . ."

But on his last visit, Peter had lost his shadow. He had come to get it back.

"Well done, Tink, you've found it," Peter whispered when Tinker Bell discovered his shadow in a drawer. But the shadow was in no hurry to be caught.

It flitted and skittered around the room!

Peter charged after it, making such a racket that Wendy immediately woke up.

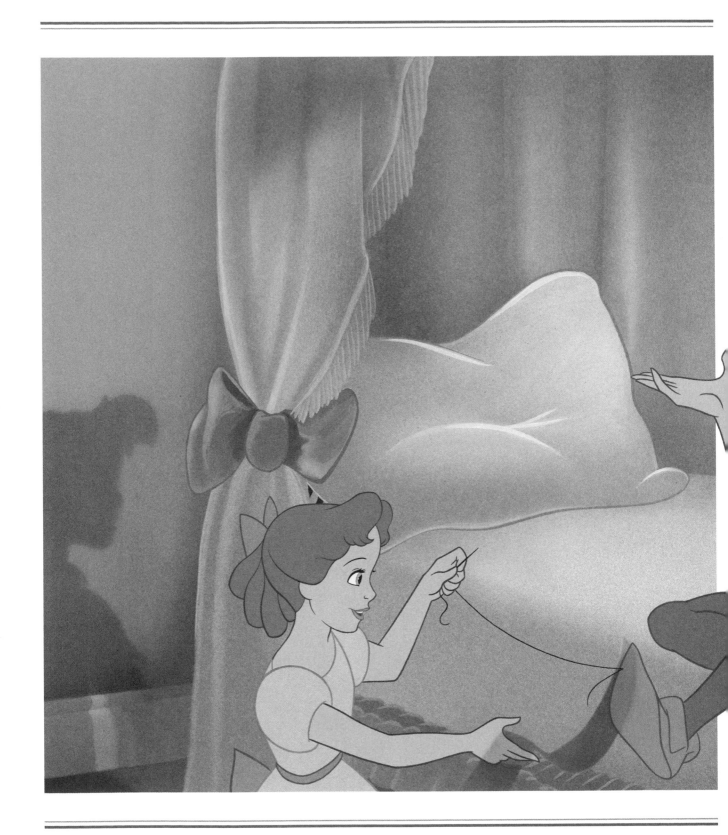

Finally, Peter caught his shadow. He tried to reattach it, but it just wouldn't stick. Wendy offered to sew it on.

"Oh, Peter, I knew you would come," she said as she sewed.

"Tonight's my last night in the nursery. I have to grow up tomorrow," Wendy added.

"But that means no more stories!" Peter cried.

"I won't have it! Come on, we're going to Never Land. You'll never grow up there."

Wendy quickly woke her brothers. Peter Pan sprinkled some of Tinker Bell's pixie dust over the children and told them to think happy thoughts.

"We're flying!" Wendy, John, and Michael shouted as they followed Peter and Tinker Bell out the nursery window. They soared over the rooftops of London. Peter laughed as he pointed up into the sky.

"There it is, Wendy. Never Land. Second star to the right and straight on till morning,"

he said.

Finally, Never Land appeared. On a ship below, a pirate named Captain Hook was busy scheming with his first mate, Mr. Smee.

Peter had chopped off Hook's hand in a sword fight and fed it to a crocodile. The Crocodile thought it was delicious, and he followed the pirate everywhere, hoping for another bite.

Hook wanted revenge on Peter Pan!

Suddenly, Captain Hook looked up and saw Peter flying in the clouds. He quickly shot a cannonball at Peter and the children. Luckily, it zoomed by, and they didn't get hurt.

"Quick, Tink! Take Wendy and the boys to the island," Peter yelled.

While Peter distracted Hook, Tinker Bell hurried toward the island. She flew so fast that Wendy, John, and Michael fell far behind. The fairy thought Peter was spending too much time with Wendy. She was jealous, and she had a plan.

Tinker Bell went to see the Lost Boys. She told the boys that Peter wanted them to shoot Wendy out of the sky.

The Lost Boys grabbed their slingshots.

"Ready . . . aim . . . fire!" they shouted.

Rocks flew everywhere. They hit Wendy and sent her tumbling from the sky.

Fortunately, Peter arrived in time to save her. But he was very angry with Tink. He banished her for a whole week!

While John and Michael played with the Lost Boys, Peter took Wendy to visit the mermaids in the lagoon.

Suddenly, Peter spotted Captain Hook and Smee.

They had kidnapped Tiger Lily, the Indian chief's daughter, and tied her to a rock in the middle of the water.

Peter revealed himself and challenged Hook to a duel. As they fought, the tide got closer and closer to Tiger Lily's head. Finally, Peter backed Captain Hook into the water, where the Crocodile snapped its jaws, waiting for another taste. Hook shouted and swam away as quickly as possible.

Peter swooped down and rescued Tiger Lily. He took her safely back to her village, where there was a great celebration in his honor.

The only person who didn't celebrate was Tinker Bell, who was very angry at being banished.

Tinker Bell was so upset that she didn't even notice Smee sneaking up behind her. He shoved her in his cap and took her to Captain Hook.

"We sail in the morning,"

Hook told Tinker Bell.

He promised to take Wendy with him if Tink would tell him where Peter's hideout was. With Tinker Bell's help, Captain Hook found his way to Peter's hideout. The pirates surrounded the tree and waited for the Lost Boys to come out.

"Captain Hook found his way to Peter's hideout."

Meanwhile, inside Peter's hideout, all was cozy and quiet. Wendy tucked the boys into bed and sang a song about the wonders of a real mother.

By the time Wendy finished singing, John and Michael were so homesick that they wanted to leave for London at once. Even the Lost Boys wanted to go.

"By the time Wendy finished singing, John and Michael were so homesick . . ."

But Peter Pan did not want to leave Never Land.

"Go back and grow up!" he said stubbornly. "I'm warnin' you, once you've grown up, you can never come back!"

One by one, the boys walked out of Peter's hideout . . .
right into the arms of the waiting pirates!

"Now to take care of Master Peter Pan!" Hook chuckled as he lowered a beautifully wrapped package into the hideout.

Inside, Peter Pan picked up the package. He was just untying the bow when Tinker Bell appeared. She flew at the box, pulling it as far from Peter as she could. Suddenly, the gift began to smoke.

And then . . .
KABOOM!

Back on the pirate ship, Wendy refused to join Captain Hook.

"Join me or walk the plank!"

Hook cried.

So with tears trickling down her cheeks, Wendy walked the plank. She took one step, then another, closer and closer to the edge, until finally . . . she jumped!

But there was no splash! Peter had saved Wendy just in the nick of time.

"This time you've gone too far!"

Peter shouted at Hook.

As Hook and Peter began to duel, John, Michael, and the Lost Boys climbed to the crow's nest. The Lost Boys threw rocks at the pirates. John even hit them on the head with his umbrella.

One by one, the pirates were defeated.

All except Hook, who was still fighting Peter.

Peter and Hook battled it out on the ship's yardarm, which had swung over the water.

Peter grabbed Hook's sword, but then decided to let him go.

But the pirate had been humiliated. He took a swipe at Peter, lost his balance, and plunged into the water, right into the jaws of the Crocodile!

Peter took control of Hook's ship. Wendy and the rest of the children cheered. "Hooray for Captain Pan!"

"Could you tell me, sir, where we're sailing?" Wendy asked with a smile.

"To London, madam," Peter replied.

Tinker Bell sprinkled the ship with pixie dust, and soon it rose into the air. Below them, Never Land disappeared.

As they approached London, Wendy and her brothers said good-bye to Peter and the Lost Boys. They knew they would never forget this adventure!

At home, Wendy's mother shook her awake. She had fallen asleep by the window. As Wendy and her parents peered out at the sky, a ship sailed across the moon.

"You know," Mr. Darling said, his arm around his daughter, "I have the strangest feeling I've seen that ship before . . . a long time ago."

And, indeed, he had.

"There she is, a full-grown lady."

—*Jock*

LADY AND THE TRAMP

"IT'S FOR YOU, DARLING. MERRY Christmas!" Jim Dear said as he handed his wife a pink-striped boxed. Inside was a little brown puppy.

Darling took one look at the puppy and decided to call her Lady. Lady was happy in her new home. She slept in the same room as Jim Dear and Darling. She romped in the yard. And she kept watch over the house.

When Lady was older, Jim Dear and Darling gave her a collar with a name tag. Lady proudly showed her new blue collar to her friends Jock and Trusty.

"There she is, a full-grown lady,"

Jock said.

Lady felt like the luckiest dog in the whole world.

Tramp lived in the neighborhood, too. But he didn't have a warm home and a family. He lived on the streets. Tramp loved scrounging for scraps and helping his friends escape the dogcatcher.

One day, Tramp overheard Jock and Trusty telling Lady that Jim Dear and Darling were expecting a baby. Lady was confused.

"What's a baby?" Lady asked her friends.

"Just a cute little bundle . . . of trouble," Tramp said. "Remember, when a baby moves in, the dog moves out."

Lady's life was about to change.

The baby came on a rainy April day. Jim Dear and Darling were thrilled with their new little boy. Lady liked the baby, too. "We're going to be all right," she said to herself. "Tramp was wrong. Nothing has changed."

Not long after, Jim Dear and Darling decided to take a trip. Jim Dear's aunt Sarah came to look after the baby. She brought her two cats with her.

"*Lady liked the baby, too.*"

Aunt Sarah was not very nice to Lady. Her two cats were not very nice, either. They made a mess of the house and pretended that Lady had caused the trouble.

"Oh, that wicked animal!" Aunt Sarah cried.

Aunt Sarah took Lady straight to the pet store.

"I want a muzzle, a good strong muzzle," she said.

The muzzle scared Lady. She jumped off the counter and ran out the door. She ran and ran.

Soon some big mean dogs started to chase her. Lady was terrified. Luckily, Tramp heard all the barking and raced to Lady's rescue.

"Oh, you poor kid," Tramp said, looking at Lady's muzzle.

"We've got to get this off. Come on."

Tramp took Lady to the zoo. Maybe one of the animals there could help her. The apes, the alligator, and the hyena were no help at all. Then Lady and Tramp found the beaver. He loved to chew and soon bit right through the muzzle's strap.

That night, Tramp took Lady to supper at Tony's Restaurant. Tramp's friend Tony liked Lady and fed the pair his specialty—spaghetti with meatballs!

Tramp and Lady accidentally ate the same spaghetti noodle. The next thing they knew, they were kissing.

Lady and Tramp were falling in love.

After dinner, the happy pair walked to the top of a hill that overlooked their town. They gazed up at the large full moon that shone over the twinkling lights of the town. It was a beautiful night.

Soon the two dogs fell asleep under the stars.

The next morning, on the way home, Tramp and Lady passed a farmyard.

"Ever chased chickens?" Tramp asked. He couldn't resist. Lady did not like the idea, but she followed him anyway. The chickens ran around, squawking. Feathers flew everywhere.

"Hey, what's going on in there?"

the farmer called.

Lady and Tramp ran away as fast as they could. They splashed through a stream and over ditches. But Tramp soon discovered that Lady wasn't behind him.

She had run into the dogcatcher and was taken to the dog pound!

Lady's eyes filled with tears as the door of her cell clanged shut behind her.

Lady was scared at the dog pound. But soon the dogcatcher came for her. Reading her collar, he found out where she lived.

"You're too nice a girl to be in this place," he said. He called Aunt Sarah, who came to pick up Lady. She was very upset with Lady for running away.

At home, Aunt Sarah chained Lady to the doghouse in the backyard.

"Stay there," Aunt Sarah said. "Don't you make any noise or I'll send you back to that pound."

Lady was so sad even Jock and Trusty could not cheer her up.

Just then Tramp arrived. He had brought Lady a big juicy bone.

Lady was angry with him.

She thought Tramp had only looked out for himself and had let her get caught. "It's all your fault!" she cried.

Tramp tried to explain himself.

"I thought you were right behind me, honest," he said.

"Good-bye. And take this with you," Lady said, kicking the bone Tramp had brought for her.

Lady was so unhappy that she lay down and cried. Suddenly, she noticed two glinting eyes. A rat was creeping into the baby's room! Lady couldn't chase it because of the chain. She could only bark.

"Stop that," Aunt Sarah called. "Hush."

"A rat was creeping into the baby's room!"

Tramp heard Lady's frantic barking and rushed back. "What's wrong, Pidge?" he asked.

"A rat! Upstairs, in the baby's room!" Lady cried.

Tramp ran into the house. He had to catch that rat before it hurt the baby! Growling, Tramp lunged at the large rat.

Meanwhile, Lady barked with all her might and pulled on the heavy chain. At last the chain broke free. Lady ran inside to help Tramp. She couldn't let anything happen to the baby!

"She couldn't let anything happen to the baby."

Lady burst into the baby's room just as Tramp chased the rat under the bassinet. In the chaos, the bassinet tipped over. The baby started to cry. Lady watched as Tramp caught the rat.

The baby was safe!

The baby's crying had woken Aunt Sarah. Rushing into the nursery, she was angry to find Lady and Tramp. She didn't see the rat and thought the dogs were hurting the baby. She called the dogcatcher to come for Tramp.

Soon the dogcatcher arrived. He threw Tramp in his wagon and drove away.

Just then, Jim Dear and Darling came home.

Aunt Sarah tried to tell them what a naughty dog Lady was, but Jim didn't believe her. Lady was barking. He knew that meant something was wrong. Lady led him to the nursery. She lifted the curtain to show them that Tramp had caught the rat and saved the baby.

Outside, Jock and Trusty had a plan to stop the dogcatcher's wagon.

They barked loudly, scaring the horses.

The wagon crashed. Tramp was safe. Jim Dear and Lady soon arrived to take him home.

The next Christmas Eve, Jock and Trusty stopped by to see Lady, Tramp—and their four puppies.

"They've got their mother's eyes," Trusty said.

"There's a bit of their father in them, too," Jock said.

Everyone was happy that Tramp had become part of the family.

"I want to stay in the jungle. I'm not afraid. I can look after myself."

—*Mowgli*

the
JUNGLE
BOOK

BAGHEERA THE PANTHER was walking through the jungle one day when he heard a strange cry. He walked to the river and found a Man-cub floating in a broken boat. The nearest Man-village was far away, and the cub needed a mother. Bagheera took the boy to a wolf family's den.

"We will call him Mowgli and raise him as our own," the wolves said. And so it was that Mowgli came to be raised in the jungle.

Over time, Mowgli grew into a boy. The wolves could no longer protect him from the dangers of the jungle. The tiger, Shere Khan, was one of these dangers. Shere Khan hated humans and wanted nothing more than to get rid of Mowgli.

One night the wolves held a council. "The Man-cub can no longer stay with the pack," Akela, the leader of the wolves, said. "The strength of the pack is no match for the tiger."

"Perhaps I can be of help," Bagheera said. "I know a Man-village where he'll be safe."

So it was decided. Bagheera would take Mowgli there.

"Shere Khan hated humans . . ."

The next day, Bagheera invited Mowgli to take a walk in the jungle.

As it grew darker, Mowgli started to feel sleepy.

He wanted to turn back, but Bagheera explained that he couldn't return to the wolf pack. They were going to the nearest Man-village instead.

As night fell, Bagheera and Mowgli stopped and curled up underneath a large tree to sleep. Suddenly, Kaa the snake dropped down from the branches overhead. Kaa's tail coiled around Mowgli.

When Bagheera woke up and saw what was happening, he hit Kaa on the head. Kaa slithered away, grumbling to himself.

The next day, Bagheera and Mowgli woke up to the ground shaking. A patrol of elephants, led by Colonel Hathi, marched by. Mowgli got down on all fours and joined the parade.

"I'll have no Man-cub in my jungle," Colonel Hathi declared.

"The Man-cub is with me," Bagheera interrupted. "I'm taking him to the Man-village."

Bagheera wanted to take Mowgli to the Man-village right away, before anything else could happen to him.

But Mowgli refused. He held on tightly to a small tree. Finally, Bagheera gave up.

"From now on, you're on your own!" Bagheera shouted as he walked off.

Mowgli sat down with his head hung low until he heard sounds coming from a nearby bush.

It was Baloo the bear.

Baloo saw that Mowgli needed some lessons on how to survive in the jungle. He taught the Man-cub everything he knew, like how to find delicacies such as bananas, coconuts, and ants!

"He taught the Man-cub everything he knew . . ."

The new friends spent the afternoon doing what Baloo liked best: nothing but eating and relaxing.

Little did Mowgli know, Bagheera was always close by, making sure no harm came to them.

As Mowgli and Baloo played, they ran into a group of monkeys. They grabbed Mowgli by the arms and began to swing through the treetops.

Baloo shouted at the monkeys, but he could not stop them from taking Mowgli.

Bagheera heard the shouting and ran to Baloo. He and Baloo had to save their Man-cub! The monkeys took Mowgli to an ancient temple. Their leader, King Louie, wanted to meet the Man-cub.

He also wanted Mowgli to teach him how to make fire!

Up above, Baloo and Bagheera watched the monkeys. They had to find a way into the monkeys' temple. Baloo had an idea.

"They had to find a way into the monkeys' temple."

Baloo disguised himself as a monkey and entered the temple, dancing and singing. King Louie took Baloo by the hand and crossed the temple's courtyard, swinging to the jungle beat.

While Baloo distracted King Louie, Bagheera tried to rescue Mowgli.

But every time he got close to the Man-cub, Mowgli moved farther and farther away.

Suddenly, Baloo's costume fell off.

"It's Baloo the bear!"
a monkey screamed.

At that moment, King Louie's temple started to crumble. Baloo asked King Louie to help him hold up the temple's roof.

As soon as King Louie was in place, Baloo let go of his end and ran away into the jungle with Mowgli and Bagheera.

That night, Bagheera explained to Baloo that Mowgli was in danger in the jungle.

But when Baloo tried to convince Mowgli that he belonged in the Man-village, Mowgli grew upset. Baloo had promised that the Man-cub could stay in the jungle with him.

Turning his back on Baloo and Bagheera, Mowgli ran away.

Later, Shere Khan overheard Bagheera say that Mowgli had run deeper into the jungle.

He had been waiting patiently for an opportunity to get the Man-cub, but Bagheera had been protecting him. If Mowgli was alone, this might be his chance!

Meanwhile, Mowgli had run into Kaa again. The python wrapped the Man-cub in his coils and began to squeeze.

Suddenly, Kaa felt a tug on his tail. It was Shere Khan!

Shere Khan flexed his claws. He wanted Kaa to give him the Man-cub.

Kaa had no choice but to agree. There was just one problem.

While he had been talking to Shere Khan, Mowgli had managed to escape!

Mowgli ran through the jungle until he came upon a flock of vultures. The vultures thought the Man-cub was a strange-looking bird and decided to keep him company.

Suddenly, there was a terrible roar.

Shere Khan pounced from the shadows!

Mowgli turned to face the tiger, who was suddenly yanked backward!

Baloo had arrived and was holding on to Shere Khan's tail. The vultures picked up Mowgli and flew him to safety as Baloo fought off the tiger.

The sky darkened and a bolt of lightning struck a nearby dead tree, setting it on fire.

Mowgli quickly grabbed a blazing branch and stormed toward Shere Khan.

Mowgli tied the burning branch to Shere Khan's tail. There was nothing the tiger feared more than fire! The tiger cried out in terror and ran away.

As the vultures flew down to congratulate the Man-cub, they found Mowgli kneeling beside his dear friend Baloo.

Shere Khan had hit him hard, and he was not moving.

Mowgli sat at his friend's side. The last time they had spoken, he had yelled at Baloo. He hoped he would have a chance to apologize.

After a long while, Baloo opened his eyes. He sat up and acted like nothing had happened.

Mowgli was glad his friend was okay!

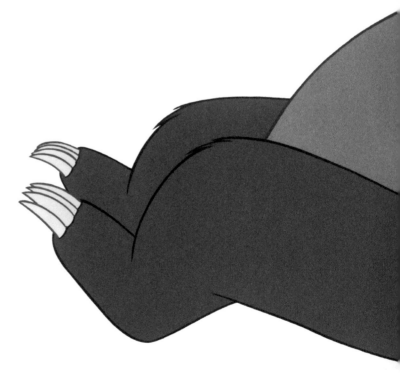

Shere Khan had been scared away, but he had not been defeated.

Sadly, Mowgli realized that his friends were right. The jungle was a dangerous place for him. It was time to go to the Man-village with Baloo and Bagheera.

As they neared the village, Mowgli noticed a pretty girl around his age fetching water from the river's edge.

Baloo and Bagheera watched as Mowgli ran to help the girl carry her jug, full of water. As Mowgli followed her into the Man-village, he turned around to give his animal friends one last smile.

Baloo and Bagheera were sad to see their little friend go, but they were happy that he'd found a place where he belonged. With one last look at Mowgli, the friends returned to the jungle once more, arm in arm.

"We are all connected in
the great Circle of Life."

—Mufasa

the
LION KING

THE HOT AFRICAN SUN rose on an amazing sight. Giraffes, zebras, elephants, and other animals of all kinds were gathered at Pride Rock. This was an important day.

King Mufasa and Queen Sarabi watched as Rafiki the wise baboon presented their newborn son to the kingdom. The animals cheered and bowed before Prince Simba.

But one family member didn't attend the celebration—Mufasa's brother, Scar. Scar was angry that he was no longer next in line to be king.

Mufasa and his steward, Zazu, went to ask Scar why he had missed the presentation of Simba.

"Oh, it must have slipped my mind," Scar sneered as he walked away.

Simba grew into a playful and curious cub. Early one morning, Mufasa took Simba to the top of Pride Rock.

"Everything that the light touches is our kingdom," he told his son.

"Wow!" Simba cried. "But what about that shadowy place?"

"You must never go across the border, Simba," Mufasa said sternly.

"Simba grew into a playful and curious cub."

"But I thought a king can do whatever he wants," Simba said.

"There's more to being king than getting your way all the time," Mufasa explained. "You need to respect all creatures.

"We are all connected in the great Circle of Life."

Simba tried to listen, but he was too busy practicing his pounce. Just then, Zazu arrived with important news. Hyenas had crossed into the Pride Lands! Mufasa ordered Zazu to take Simba home, and he ran off to battle the hyenas.

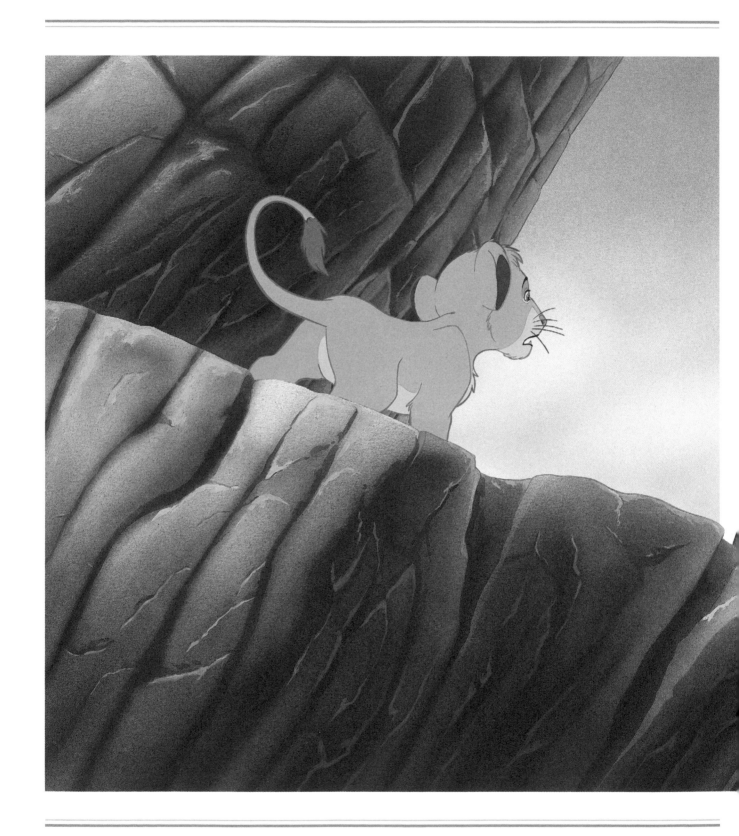

Back at home, Simba went to see his uncle, Scar.

"My dad just showed me the whole kingdom," the cub bragged.

"And I'm gonna rule it all!"

"Did he show you that place beyond the border?" Scar asked slyly. "Only the bravest of the lions would dare go to an elephant graveyard."

Simba didn't see his uncle's evil trap. He decided to show his father what a brave cub he could be.

Simba set out to find his best friend, Nala. She was lying with their mothers on a rock nearby.

"Mom, can Nala and I go to this great place . . . near the water hole?" Simba fibbed.

"As long as Zazu goes with you," Sarabi answered

"We've got to ditch Zazu!" Simba whispered to Nala.

"We're really going to an elephant graveyard."

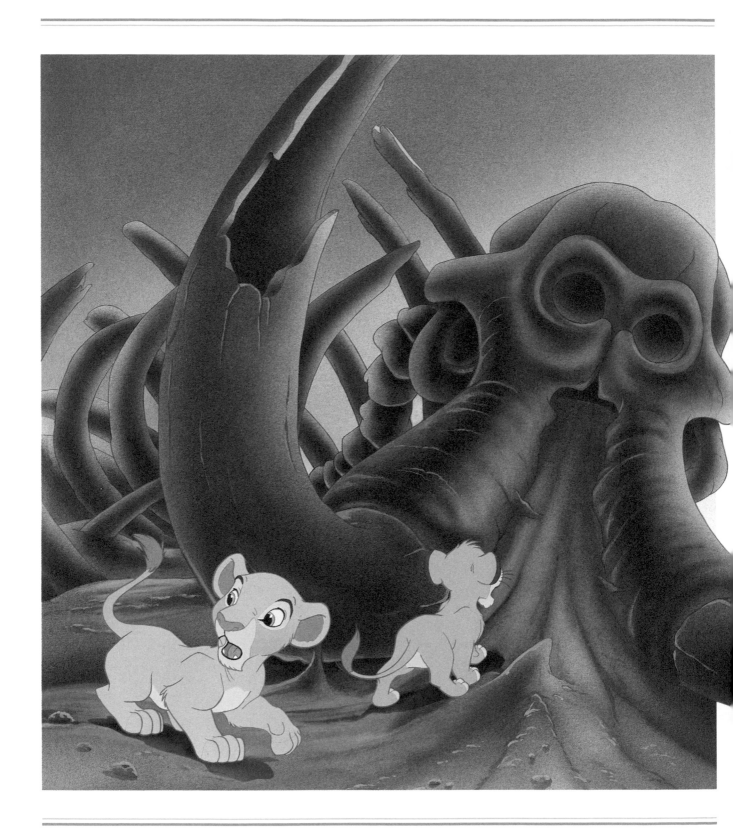

Simba and Nala laughed as they ran in and out of animal herds to escape from Zazu. Finally, they lost him. Together the cubs played, tumbling and rolling. With a thump, they landed next to a huge elephant skull.

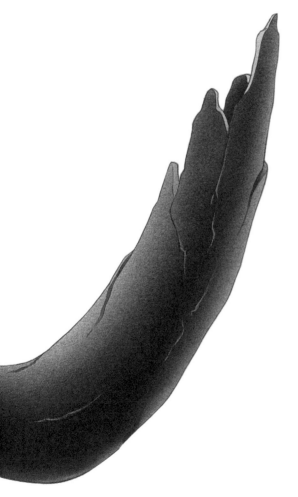

Zazu caught up with them, but it was too late.

Banzai, Shenzi, and Ed, three drooling hyenas with sharp teeth, surrounded them!

The hyenas grabbed Zazu first. Then Shenzi tried to catch Nala, but Simba swiped his claws across the hyena's cheek.

Suddenly, a tremendous roar shook the ground. It was Mufasa! His giant paws struck the hyenas.

"If you ever come near my son again . . ." he growled.

The hyenas ran away before Mufasa could finish.

"The hyenas grabbed Zazu . . ."

Mufasa scolded his son on the way home. "You disobeyed me, Simba," he said.

"I was just trying to be brave, like you, Dad," Simba said softly.

"Being brave doesn't mean you go looking for trouble," Mufasa replied.

Then Mufasa told Simba that the kings of the past looked down on them from the stars above. "They will always be there to guide you, and so will I," he said.

Scar was angry when the hyenas told him that Simba had escaped. But he quickly came up with a new plan to get rid of Simba and his father.

"I will be king!" he cried.

The next day, Scar found Simba. "Your father has a surprise for you," he said. Scar led Simba down into a steep gorge and told him to wait there.

Scar signaled the hyenas to frighten a herd of wildebeests. The panicked animals stampeded right toward Simba! Mufasa looked into the gorge and saw his son.

Mufasa leaped down, grabbed Simba, and tossed him up onto a ledge.

Simba was safe, but Mufasa was still in danger. As he tried to climb away from the stampede, the rocks began to crumble beneath him.

As he struggled up the cliff, Mufasa saw Scar.

"Brother, help me!" Mufasa cried.

Scar dug his sharp claws into Mufasa's paws and whispered, "Long live the king!"

Then he let his brother go. Mufasa disappeared beneath the herd below. Simba only saw his father fall. When the stampede was gone, he ran to Mufasa. He tried to wake him up, but the Lion King was dead.

"Long live the king!"

Scar went to Simba's side. "If it weren't for you, your father would still be alive!" he said. "Run away and never return!"

Heartbroken, poor Simba ran away as fast as he could. Scar sent the hyenas out to kill Simba, but the cub escaped them once more.

Scar was certain that Simba was dead. He went back to Pride Rock and told everyone the news.

"It is with a heavy heart that I become your new king!" he said.

Everyone in the Pride Lands mourned for their beloved king Mufasa and for Simba.

Meanwhile, Simba was far away from the Pride Lands, lost in the desert. Exhausted and unable to go any farther, Simba slumped to the ground.

After a long while, he awoke. Everything around him looked different. There were trees, grass, and flowers instead of desert.

A meerkat named Timon and a warthog named Pumbaa had taken him to their home. Thanking them, Simba stood up and started to leave.

Pumbaa asked Simba where he was from, but Simba didn't want to answer. "I did something terrible . . . but I don't want to talk about it," Simba said.

"You gotta put your troubles behind you, kid," Timon said.

"No past, no futures, no worries . . . *hakuna matata!*"

Simba thought for a moment and decided to stay with his new friends.

Years passed, and Simba grew into a young lion. One day, Pumbaa was chasing a bug when a fierce lioness sprang at him from the tall grass. He screamed and ran away, but he got stuck beneath a fallen tree.

"She's going to eat me!"

he squealed.

Simba heard his friend's cries and rushed to help.

As Simba wrestled with the lioness, he realized she was his old friend Nala.

"You're alive!" she said happily. "That means you're the king!"

Nala told Simba how Scar had destroyed the Pride Lands. "Simba, if you don't do something, everyone will starve!" she said.

"I can't go back," Simba said angrily, and he turned and walked away.

Simba thought about what Nala had said. "I won't go back," he said to himself. "It won't change anything."

Just then, Simba heard chanting coming from the jungle. Rafiki the baboon walked toward him.

"If you want to see your father again, look down there," Rafiki said, pointing to the pool of water next to them.

Simba saw the face of his father staring back at him. "You see?" Rafiki said.

"He lives in you!"

Simba looked up to the sky. He saw his father's face in the stars and heard Mufasa's voice.

"Look inside yourself, Simba. Remember who you are. You are my son and the one true king."

The next morning, Rafiki found Nala, Timon, and Pumbaa. He told them that Simba had returned to the Pride Lands.

When Simba reached the Pride Lands, he was saddened by what he saw.

His homeland, which had once been green and beautiful, had turned barren under Scar's rule. Bravely, Simba continued on his journey.

Simba arrived at Pride Rock and let out a roar that shook the earth. Scar was surprised and frightened. He thought the hyenas had killed Simba long before.

"This is my kingdom!" Simba shouted. "Step down, Scar."

Scar ordered his hyenas to attack. They surrounded Simba and drove him to the edge of a cliff.

Simba grabbed at the rocks with his claws as Scar stood above him. "That's just the way your father looked before I killed him," Scar snarled.

Simba realized that it was Scar who had killed Mufasa. With new strength, Simba lunged onto the rock and attacked Scar.

At that moment, Nala, Timon, and Pumbaa arrived, and a battle broke out on Pride Rock.

This time, Simba trapped Scar at the steep edge of Pride Rock.

Sparing Scar's life, Simba ordered his uncle to run away and never return.

Scar pretended to leave, but then turned and lunged at Simba. Simba swiped his great paw, and Scar fell to his death in the gorge below.

Simba took his rightful place as the Lion King, and the Pride Lands flourished once again.

Soon all the animals gathered at Pride Rock to celebrate the birth of Simba and Nala's cub. The Circle of Life would continue.

Collection copyright © 2016 Disney Enterprises, Inc.

Individual copyrights and credits for works included in this collection:

"Pinocchio" originally published as *Pinocchio* copyright © 2011 Disney Enterprises, Inc. Based on the book by Carlo Collodi.

"Peter Pan" originally published as *Peter Pan* copyright © 2011 Disney Enterprises, Inc.

"Lady and the Tramp" originally published as *Lady and the Tramp: A Read-Aloud Storybook* copyright © 2000 Disney Enterprises, Inc. Retold by Debbie Weissman.

"The Jungle Book" originally published as *The Jungle Book* copyright © 2011 Disney Enterprises, Inc. Based on the Mowgli stories in *The Jungle Book* and *The Second Jungle Book* by Rudyard Kipling.

"The Lion King" originally published as *The Lion King: A Read-Aloud Storybook* copyright © 1999 Disney Enterprises, Inc. Retold by Liza Baker.

All artwork by the Disney Storybook Art Team

For information address Disney Press, 1101 Flower Street, Glendale, California 91201.

Printed in the United States of America

First Hardcover Edition, September 2016

Library of Congress Control Number: 2016936334

1 3 5 7 9 10 8 6 4 2

ISBN 978-1-4847-8960-5

FAC-008598-16204

For more Disney Press fun, visit www.disneybooks.com

SUSTAINABLE FORESTRY INITIATIVE   Certified Sourcing
www.sfiprogram.org
SFI-00993
This Label Applies to Text Stock Only